Fun on the Farm

AT THE DAIRY FARM

By George Pendergast

Gareth Stevens
PUBLISHING

Please visit our website, www.garethstevens.com. For a free color catalog of all our high-quality books, call toll free 1-800-542-2595 or fax 1-877-542-2596.

Cataloging-in-Publication Data

Names: Pendergast, George.
Title: At the dairy farm / George Pendergast.
Description: New York : Gareth Stevens Publishing, 2017. | Series: Fun on the farm | Includes index.
Identifiers: ISBN 9781482455168 (pbk.) | ISBN 9781482455182 (library bound) | ISBN 9781482455175 (6 pack)
Subjects: LCSH: Dairy farming –Juvenile literature. | Dairy farms–Juvenile literature.
Classification: LCC SF208.P46 2017 | DDC 636.2'142–dc23

First Edition

Published in 2017 by
Gareth Stevens Publishing
111 East 14th Street, Suite 349
New York, NY 10003

Editor: Ryan Nagelhout
Designer: Laura Bowen

Photo credits: Cover, p. 1 smereka/Shutterstock.com; pp. 5, 24 Budimir Jevtic/Shutterstock.com; p. 7 Jenco van Zalk/Moment Open/Getty Images; pp. 9, 24 MaxyM/Shutterstock.com; p. 11 Australian Scenics/Photolibrary/Getty Images; p. 13 Lester Lefkowitz/Photographer's Choice/Getty Images; p. 15 NaturalBox/Shutterstock.com; pp. 17, 24 Igumnova Irina/Shutterstock.com; p. 19 Toa55/Shutterstock.com; p. 21 Gts/Shutterstock.com; p. 23 Africa Studio/Shutterstock.com.

Printed in the United States of America

CPSIA compliance information: Batch #CW17GS: For further information contact Gareth Stevens, New York, New York at 1-800-542-2595.

Contents

Some farmers do not
grow plants.
They take care of cows.

Farmers get milk
from cows.

Cows live in barns.

They walk around
in big fields.
This is called grazing.

They eat lots of grass.

Cows make milk!

Milk comes from
a cow's udder.

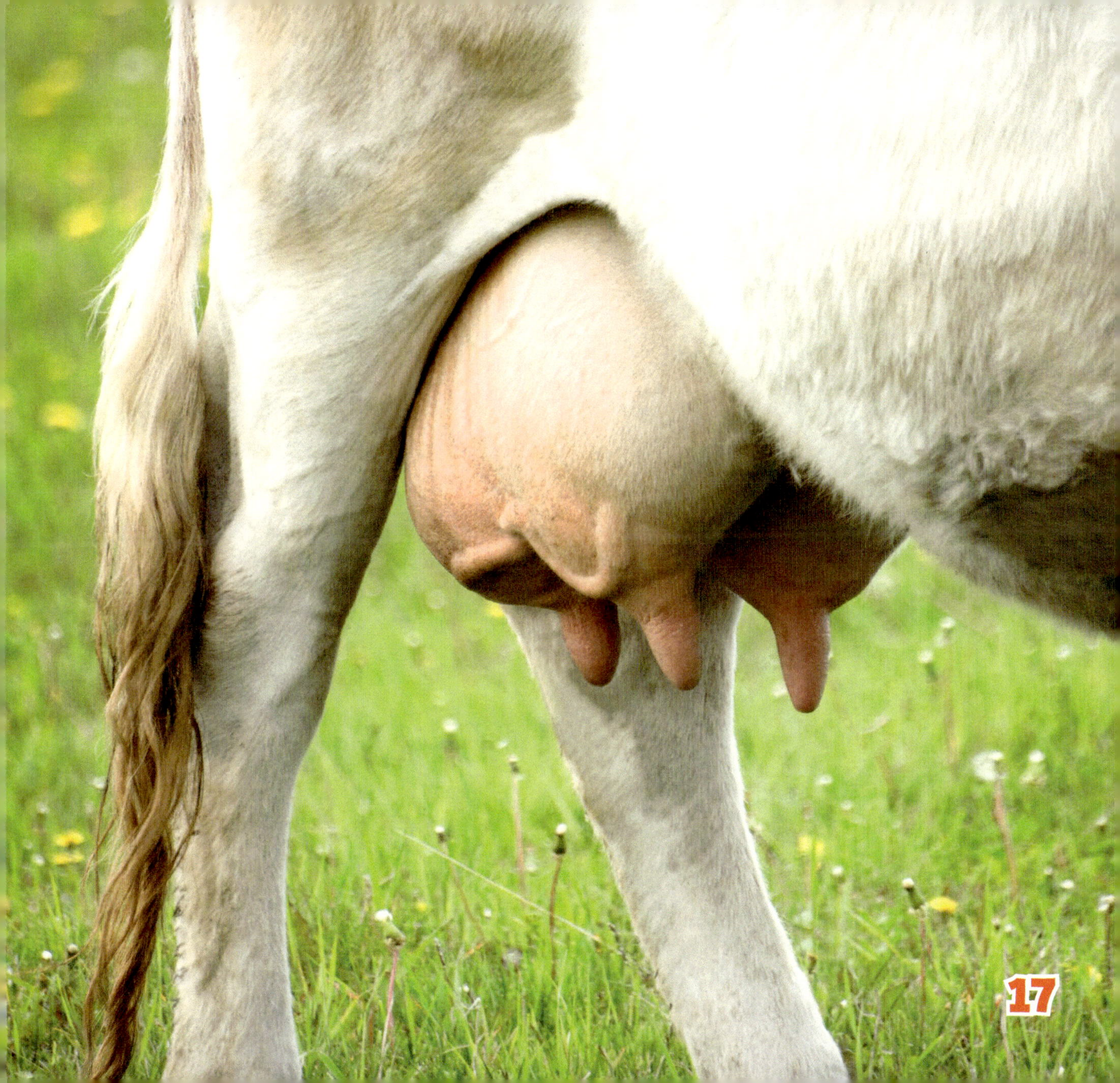

The cows are milked.

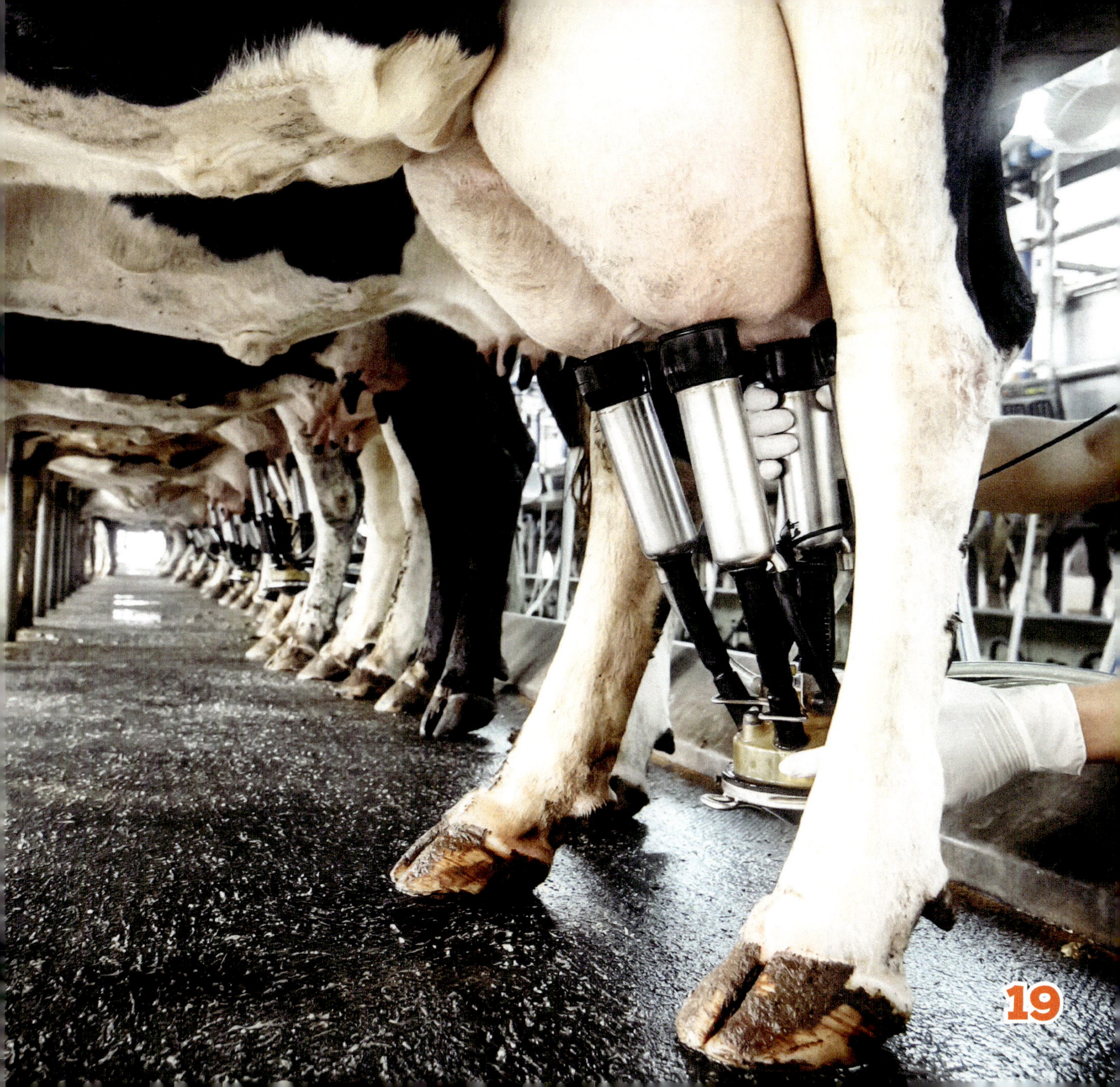

The milk can be put in bottles.

Milk is used to make other foods, too!

Words to Know

barn

cow

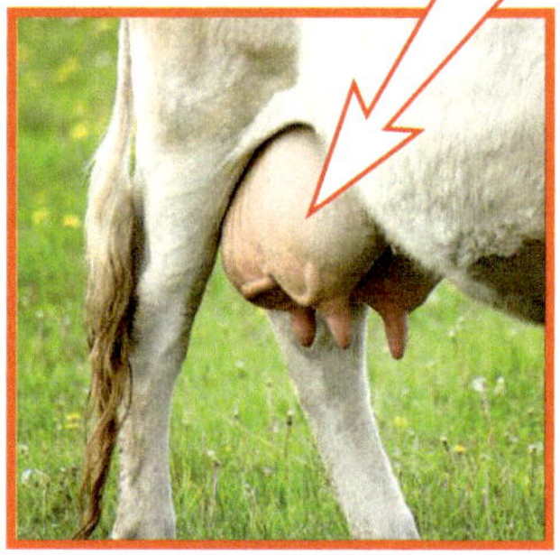
udder

Index